ROOM

by

Roger Harvey

To Sue with love and very best wishes from Roger. xx

Christmas 2015.

The right of Roger Harvey to be identified as the author of this work has been asserted by him in accordance with provisions of the Copyright, Designs and Patents Act 1988.

This material is copyright Roger Harvey 1995, 2006 and 2015. All rights reserved. No part of this material may be published or reproduced in any way without the express permission of the author. Licence to publish, copy, broadcast, adapt, or otherwise develop this material or any part of it may only be obtained from the author at roger-harvey01@btinternet.com.

First published in the United Kingdom in 2015 by Create, 140 Tabernacle Street, London EC2A 4SD.

ISBN 9781785073830

Typeset in Garamond. Cover design by Heather MacPherson at Raspberry Creative Type, Edinburgh; visit raspberrycreativetype.com.

A sleepy village in post-war Northumberland, a happy one-parent family, a quiet life in the country…but when the daughters of a retired naval officer learn he is bringing home a new wife, things look anything but shipshape. This heartwarming story, told with honesty and humour, is set in the heady days of the 1960s.

To

the memory of my mother and father

with thanks for happy days in Northumberland *then*,

and to my beloved wife Sheila

with thanks for happy days *now*.

Room for Love -- Part One

"A what?" I yelled at Elizabeth as I came in from the shops, a great sob pushing up in my throat. "A what?"

"A stepmother," repeated Elizabeth, more concerned about finishing her tea and licking jam off her fingers. "Dad's married a woman and he's bringing her here to be our stepmother. You just missed him on the 'phone from London. He sounded awfully excited—but not in the way you are. Aren't you pleased?" She continued with her tea, unimpressed by my tearful collapse into a chair.

"Oh God," I wailed, "this is terrible. It's the end of everything!"

"Don't take God's name in vain," said my tall but self-contained tormentor, "especially when I know you don't believe in Him. I believe in God. God is everywhere. He's looking at you now."

"Oh shut up!" I cried. "You don't understand. A new wife, in this house, that's what it means. He's got married and never told us 'til now! She'll hate us as much as we'll hate her. She'll think we're boring and backward and not understand how we live here. She'll want to change everything and it'll be awful!"

"Might not," reasoned Elizabeth between mouthfuls of cake. "She might be nice and make us big teas and give us money and things. Anyway, Daddy loves her even if you don't. He said so on the 'phone."

"Just shut up, will you?"

Kate burst in. I felt I must be red with shock, but she was actually white—with fury. Her grim, pale face between its curtains of dark hair made her look almost mad.

"Some scheming woman!" She howled. "She's nabbed him at that Boat Show and she's coming here to take over everything!"

"Oh Katie," I hugged my elder sister. "How is it we didn't know about this before? He must have been going out with her all this time in London. What can we do?"

"Nothing, of course." She pushed me from her, brusque and furious. "And you haven't heard the worst of it yet. She's Swedish."

"Swedish?"

"No, Bulgarian," chirped Elizabeth, "or was it Rumanian?"

"Shut up! Swedish? Swedish?"

"Does Daddy speak any Swedish?" asked Elizabeth, undaunted.

Kate sank on to a chair beside me.

"He will now," she smiled ruefully. "We'll all be speaking flaming Swedish before the year's out." She rested her chin on her hand and gave me a hollow grin. "Can you believe it, Julie? Married again—and to a Swede! She'll be some big blonde busty thing; bowled him over in middle age. She'll have him for breakfast and make our lives hell while she's doing it. It's a disaster, a bloody disaster."

"You're only swearing because Daddy's not here," smirked Elizabeth. "Daddy hates swearing, even though he was in the Navy and knows all the words. I know all the words too but I never use them."

"Shut up. Anyway," Kate went on, "it's no good getting into a state, Julie. We'll have to deal with this calmly.

He was due back tomorrow night, but he's staying an extra week so Helena can organise her things."

"Helena," I mused. "That's not a very Swedish-sounding name."

"What were you expecting," replied Kate bitterly, "Ingrid-bloody-Bergman?"

"I suppose it would be nice," I admitted, "if she turned out to be as beautiful as Ingrid Bergman."

"Nobody is as beautiful as Ingrid Bergman," put in Elizabeth, film critic and stirrer-upper. "I liked her best with short hair in *For Whom the Bell Tolls*."

"Oh shut up!" cried Kate. "Swedish, for God's sake. For one thing, the language is impossible. Have you heard any? When you speak it you have to sound as if you're being sick…"

"No, that's Dutch," interrupted Elizabeth.

"…and they're very odd people. They didn't even fight on our side in the War."

"Of course not, stupid!" Elizabeth spluttered

through a mouthful of scone. "Sweden's a neutral country. Everybody knows that. They didn't fight for *anyone* in the War."

"Well that shows them up to be a selfish lot, doesn't it?" retorted Kate.

It fell to me to try and be reasonable.

"Tell me, Kate," I asked. "How is it we've never heard of this woman? Has he been keeping her a secret all this time in London? How *could* he not have told us?"

"No, no," explained Kate. "He hasn't been as wicked as that. It all seems to have happened very quickly. Apparently he met her through this Boat Show business, they fell in love, and they've stayed down there to get married as quickly as possible. Now the deed is done, he's like a dog with two tails. Kids' stuff, isn't it? Just like in the pictures."

"Well," I hurried on, "is she beautiful? Is she rich and famous or something, living in London with all the posh people?"

"Of course not, you daftie! She'll just be some bitch

of an older woman who sees an easy sit-down in the country here with three stepdaughters to slave on after her. From what I understand, she's a retired yachtswoman."

"Retired?" queried Elizabeth. "Does that mean she's very old?"

"No, it means she's given up the sea to go fishing for a husband on dry land…and she's found one."

"A yachtswoman." I allowed myself a little smile. "Well, I can see how they must have fallen for each other."

"Exactly." Kate's fury was undiminished. "It'll be intolerable. She'll be a brawny brute who takes cold showers, then they'll be scrubbing floors together and polishing the brass and having us all running round like a crew of sailors: far worse than Dad on his own. Everything'll be cold and bare and Scandinavian. She'll probably sack Mrs. Patterson—or worse, keep her on and treat her like a lowly servant while she plays Lady of the Manor. Well, she won't like it. Ha! Just wait 'til she sees how small and pathetic this place is, how little money there is, how difficult we can be, and how there's mud up to your knees every Winter and no London parties to go to. Anyway," Kate blazed up again, "I'm not having it, I tell you. She needn't come here trying to rule the roost and telling us all what to do. If the worst comes to the worst I'll make Richard take me to Gretna Green and we'll be married in a week!"

"No, Katie," I wailed. "Don't be silly; you can't do that. We need you. You said we had to be calm about it. Now, let's just sit down and think and try to see it Dad's way."

"There's nothing more to see—apart from the woman herself; and that'll be soon enough. Don't forget he's bringing her here next week."

"Oh, blast him!" I exclaimed, losing my reason again. "It's horrible. They're going to live together here as man and wife where Mother and he set up house. Don't you just detest it? Oh, you're right Kate: I hate her already. It's horrible, it's horrible."

"No it isn't," said Elizabeth, finally swallowing the last of her tea. "We're going to have a new Mum. Everyone else we know has a Mum; it's time *we* had one. I don't care if she *is* Swedish; I like her being Swedish, it's exciting. We might go abroad for our holidays now and learn a foreign language and eat Swedish food and things like that. You two, you just don't understand Daddy."

At that moment, we didn't—and I think that hurt us more than anything else. I went to bed and couldn't get to sleep, turning all this over in my mind, turning over my whole life, turning, turning, turning. How had I come to this night when I couldn't sleep for worry?

I was born after the end of the Second World War, so I was fortunate never to know its horrors or excitements at first hand—yet I seemed to grow up in its shadow as my two sisters and I lived with our father in the quiet Northumbrian village of Felton. The disused RAF airfield at Eshott, once home to Spitfires, held a potent atmosphere in its weed-strewn perimeter and oil-stained, tyre-streaked tarmac. One of my first boyfriends taught me to drive there, whizzing up and down the old runways in a Ford Anglia, and as I set the car going faster and faster I used to pretend I was pulling back on the steering-column and lifting my make-believe aircraft up over the wide fields with the grey North Sea swinging into view only a few miles ahead…but I'll tell you more about Alan and his Ford Anglia later.

The airfield anchored real-life war stories in our young imaginations. According to our father's oft-told tales, Spitfires from Northumberland had beaten back an invading force of German bombers, downing them in the sea beyond the Farne Islands: this in our own relatively forgotten part of the country when the main Battle of Britain was being fought over Kent. Dad never tired of telling us how he himself wished he had gone into the RAF instead of the Navy, thinking it much more glamorous than tramping about the oceans in a dull grey ship. Privately, I thought he had been very lucky not to have been a pilot, since he would almost certainly have been killed. He used to laughingly agree when I pointed out how bad he was at fairground shooting galleries; he couldn't have hit a barn door at forty paces, never mind an enemy fighter coming out of the sun. Fortunately for all of us, the hostilities were over and the worst he had to do was blaze away with a farmer's gun at the rats which sometimes came into our garden—I knew he never liked killing them, which is perhaps why he always missed—but the war still seemed to affect our lives. Throughout the 'Fifties and into the early 'Sixties we unconsciously dressed like Land Army girls and still called our groceries 'the rations'; when Dad took us to the cinema in Newcastle (which of course we always called 'the pictures') it was usually to see his favourite type of war film. It was only when we first heard pop music and got a television and decided we were Beatles fans that things began to change.

Although our lives might have seemed old-fashioned and quiet compared to those of girls growing up in today's hectic world, we didn't feel disadvantaged or isolated. Felton was quiet, but it wasn't exactly the backwoods. We took the bus to school just a few miles away in the busy county town of Alnwick. Felton lay on the Great North Road and we would often be driven to the constantly developing city of Newcastle, making the trip in Dad's Morris Minor. Later he bought a large Wolseley and we really felt queens of the road in that stately dove-grey car, whooshing down to the shops in Newcastle or up to Edinburgh for a special day out. But most of all we enjoyed running more or less wild in the woods and fields and valleys around our home.

We were tomboys, although I don't think any of us could have been called mannish. When I look at photographs from that time I see three pretty girls managing to look feminine even in their rough country clothes. There we are, three sisters in the black-and-white world before television and pop stars and computers came to change everything. Kate is the eldest, a war baby three years older than me. She has the best hair-do, saved-up-for over months and created in a posh Newcastle salon where the ladies were always served real ground coffee and the elegantly dressed proprietress was always addressed as 'Miss. Thorne' and everyone seemed to have wonderfully lacquered nails. Indeed Kate's hair was the glory of the family: a rich red-brown, very thick and lustrous. Dad kept telling her it was beautiful and made us sick with jealousy. I am in the middle wearing my usual tatty trousers and a thick jumper but very shiny jodhpur boots. Then there is Elizabeth, the youngest, who got the best name because she was born in Coronation year. She used to annoy Kate and myself by reminding us her name was more famous than either of ours because it was the Queen's name and there it was on every coin minted since she had been born. We used to retaliate by making fun of her tall, thin stature and calling her 'Everest' after that other great event of 1953—but secretly I always thought Elizabeth *was* the best of our names, having a fine sweet ring to it, and indeed it did look good on every coin. My own name, Julie, I thought very plain and silly and childish.

My mother was never a major figure in my life, although I was nearly seven when she died, just after Elizabeth had been born. I remember her as a tall, glamorous, rather loud woman, not very motherly, always pre-occupied with horses and travelling the South of England in her career as a show-jumper, which she had somehow managed to continue even after having three children. This took her away from home and we grew up largely beyond her influence. She was killed in a terrible riding accident when her horse bolted into a convoy of army trucks: somehow another shadow of the War, extending our father's long loneliness over our girlhoods…and through the innocence of childhood it took us many years to realise what Dad must have suffered. We were simply used to having just a father and the dour but faithful Mrs. Patterson who 'did' for us. She didn't 'do' particularly well, but there was no-one else available or willing. Dad, retired from the Navy, used to address her as if she had been a rating and actually did tours of inspection with her, pointing out dusty shelves and spillages on the cooker. Like all sailors, he was perfectly capable of keeping the house and himself clean and shipshape and expected the same immaculate standards in others. He could have run the place himself but I suppose rightly felt it was better to have a woman's presence in the home and he must have hoped we would learn something about housekeeping from Mrs. Patterson. I don't believe we ever did.

You mustn't think Dad was a tyrant pacing the house as if he were on the bridge of a destroyer and barking orders at us all. He was kind and gentle and full of good humour and absolutely lovable. It must have been difficult for him with three daughters to bring up through school and childhood illnesses and boyfriends and everything else girlhood could throw at him, but lucky that we lived away from urban dangers and distractions and at a time when England still seemed an old-fashioned country: safe and cosy and unchanging. Even the thrill of our having boyfriends, so wildly exciting to us then, seems tame in comparison to what goes on nowadays. Elizabeth, of course, was at the age when boys were denounced as 'stupid creatures', yet had a ten-year-old's frank but dismissive interest in sex, watching Kate and her boyfriend Richard with a kind of disgusted fascination. Kate had left school and found a part-time job in a gift shop in Alnwick; Richard was a farmer's son she had met there and he was clearly in love with her, although Kate could be so cool it was difficult to know how she really felt about him. Dad called him her 'beau', which sounded silly and old-fashioned to us, but in a sense that's exactly what he was and all that he was. He bought her presents and took her to the pictures and to dances and seemed kind and affectionate yet always tongue-tied in her presence.

"All he wants is sexual intercourse," declared Elizabeth one day, "but he's too soppy to get on with it."

"Elizabeth!" I slapped her round the shoulders.

"Don't be so rude and silly."

"It's not rude and it's not silly—it's just the Facts of Life. I know all the Facts of Life. I happen to think sexual intercourse is just something messy. Rabbits have it far better than humans and I'm never going to have it."

It didn't look as if I would ever have it either. I was at an all-girls school in Alnwick and had been studying hard for my final exams. There was Alan, of course, with his Ford Anglia and his ready smile, but I didn't really 'fancy' him or imagine any kind of relationship with him other than our easygoing friendship and our interest in animals and the countryside. While all this was going on, my real ambition was to be an actress: not a highbrow stage actress learning Shakespeare, but a popular one working in films and on television. Of course I didn't know how to set about this and was too shy to ask, so it had to remain a private fantasy. I organised a makeshift theatre in the loft of our house, which we always called the 'roof room'. It really was fun up there: we built a small stage at one end and rigged up primitive lights and a sliding curtain, and with a few other boys and girls from the village we would put on plays. This went on for several years through our childhood. Kate always looked marvellous on stage but wasn't very good at remembering her lines. I found acting easy but actually preferred directing and making the theatrical most of our cramped facilities. Elizabeth thought acting was 'daft' and kept saying so, but seemed to thoroughly enjoy working the lights and curtain. The heyday of the roof room must have lasted two or three years, but like most childhood enthusiasms it fell away from us as our friends changed and we grew older—but I still used to sing and dance and recite at Christmas and make Dad roar with laughter, so I think his having three daughters was fun rather than harrowing. It might have gone on like this for ever if the world hadn't changed around us and Kate hadn't insisted that Dad should make more of his 'second career'.

Although he didn't own a yacht, Dad was a keen sailor when able to indulge in the sport with his friends; he was also an electronics expert. He had combined these interests and invented a relay system for yachting instruments. It sounded very boring and complicated to me—although Elizabeth claimed to understand it—but he assured me that most good yachts already had a relay compass over the skipper's bunk. Dad's better idea was to have relays of all the major instruments: compass, chronometer, log, barometer, wind speed and direction indicator, even an echo-sounder, and market a neatly-designed mounting with all the electronics inside it. It would be aimed at the single-handed yachtsman who couldn't afford not to see his instruments even when 'off watch' in his bunk. Dad's real genius was to minimise the wiring of all this and, with a good deal of businesss acumen, see it through to production. It was rather ahead of its time, but it was a hit at the 1963 Earl's Court Boat Show. Following that success, Dad found he had to spend more time in London, leaving us to manage the house with the dubious assistance of Mrs. Patterson. Kate, the eldest and perhaps most likely to assume a housewifely rôle, was neither very good at nor very interested in keeping house, and as Winter came it fell to me to organise most of the shopping and cooking and cleaning and washing while Dad was away. I suppose it was useful experience but I didn't enjoy it much. Worse was to come when Dad announced he would be leaving again on Boxing Day and staying in London right through to the next Boat Show at the end of January…and that was how, in early 1964, he found himself marketing his invention at Earl's Court again, and we found ourselves with a new stepmother.

* * *

The dreaded day drew nearer. The weather was intensely cold, with frosty mornings and ice-bound nights, but the sky was mostly blue and sunny with a foretaste of Spring in the air, and the sparkling countryside seemed an appropriately-lit setting for the truly dramatic start to our New Year. Nothing and no-one could hide in this brilliant blue-and-yellow light; everything would be shown up larger than life and be inescapable. I was always so much affected by invigorating weather that I couldn't help but feel a little more hopeful.

"We really should make the best of it," I said to my sisters. "You know, tidy the place up a bit so when Dad comes back with Helena they don't find us living in too much of a mess. We've still got a few days to wash the curtains and things."

"I'm not lifting a finger for this woman," said Kate haughtily. "Let her do her own housework."

Sure enough, every evening when Elizabeth and I returned from school, we found nothing had improved in the house. Poor Mrs. Patterson swept and dusted and baked scones as best she could, making no secret of being worried about her future, but she clearly didn't intend to put on any kind of show for her new mistress. On the Saturday morning when Kate was at work, Elizabeth and I had a long talk. I felt terribly anxious that despite her childish bravado and excitement, Elizabeth might suffer more emotional turmoil than either Kate or myself. After all, she was the youngest and she had a very loving, secure, tomboyish relationship with our father which I felt would certainly be altered by his marriage.

"Kate's taken this very badly," I said. "You can understand why, can't you? She knew our real Mum for ten years before she died; that's half her lifetime. She feels as if Dad has betrayed her by transferring all his affection to a woman Kate hasn't even met."

Elizabeth looked at me blankly. Was I talking 'adult's twaddle' as I had once heard her dismiss such reasoned explanation? I carried on regardless.

"But we have to be more sensible. When you think about it, there's really no reason why Dad shouldn't fall in love all over again with somebody new. It happens all the time in films and stories; it must happen all the time in real life. It just hasn't happened in our family before, that's why it feels so strange."

"Yes, it does feel strange," answered Elizabeth, suddenly sounding much more grown-up than I had expected, "but I think Kate's being very silly about it really. Of course we should have a new Mum. If Dad loves her, it doesn't mean he doesn't love us, does it?"

"No, of course it doesn't, but Kate *thinks* it might." I realised my fears for Elizabeth were largely groundless; it was Kate who would suffer the most.

"She's stupid then," declared Elizabeth.

"No, she's not stupid, and you know she's not. She's just frightened. You know what it's like when you're frightened of something. You don't really think, you just cry or run away."

"I'm not frightened. Are you?"

"No, I'm not frightened of Helena. I am a bit shy about meeting her, I suppose."

"I'm not shy. I want to talk to her in Swedish when she comes in. I've been trying to find out what's Swedish for 'welcome' but I can't find a Swedish dictionary anywhere. We could ask Dad next time he's on the 'phone, but that would spoil the surprise."

"I know Kate doesn't want to," I continued, "but we should really make the bedroom as nice as we can for them. Perhaps we could put up the Summer curtains and change the bedspread. Still, we shouldn't upset Kate more than she is already."

So I assumed the uncomfortable rôles of peacemaker and mistress of ceremonies, steering between Kate's hostile indifference and Elizabeth's childish enthusiasm. Actually, I was becoming deeply excited at the prospect of someone new in the family, surprise Swedish stepmother or not. When I thought about it, our lives were dull, and here was an opportunity for us all to blossom into something glamorous and cosmopolitan, for Dad to find love again, for us to have a new mother who might even become a new friend. I imagined, perhaps too romantically, that she would bring a whole new way of life. At the same time I wished Dad would be more open with us; would telephone more often and let us know what was happening in London and what was supposed to happen when they arrived back in the North. He hadn't even let us speak to Helena on the 'phone, which I thought was very mean of him, but he just laughed it off saying it would spoil the surprise of meeting her. At that moment, she seemed the kind of surprise I didn't want, and I began to think Kate was right when she said Dad was 'totally besotted with the woman' and that he wouldn't have a thought or a moment to spare for us ever again. However, I was soon carried away with plans for making the house as attractive as I could and for preparing a special welcome tea on the day they were to arrive. Kate did nothing, doggedly going to work in the mornings and slouching moodily in front of the fire in the evenings, refusing to help with the housework, wash her hair, or even speak to us.

Elizabeth was making a little Swedish flag from scraps of blue and yellow material and planting it in a bar of perfumed soap she had bought for Helena: a touch of feminine thoughtfulness I had never expected to see. Perhaps fortunately, Elizabeth never did discover the Swedish word for 'welcome' which she was going to carve in the soap. Instead, we adapted an old German custom we knew of putting chocolates in a guest's bedroom, and set the be-flagged soap on a dish of sweets. It looked like a tiny yacht sailing across the pillow. It felt good to be able to indulge a newly-discovered taste for making the most of a special occasion. Amongst all this bustle I went up to the roof room to find something I needed. Suddenly our makeshift theatre seemed forlorn and empty and childish. I felt certain we had given our last performance there, and came down the narrow stairs not entirely sorry to believe I had closed a long chapter of my life.

* * *

The bright weather held. Winter sunshine streamed over the countryside as we woke on the morning of Dad's arrival with Helena. Elizabeth and I had taken the day off school, but Kate went to do her usual morning's work at the shop in Alnwick. We knew they were motoring from London in Helena's car. They were sure to have left early, but even driving quickly up the Great North Road, they wouldn't be in Northumberland until after lunch.

It was fun at first, putting on what I thought was a smart skirt and jumper, marshalling my forces of Elizabeth and Mrs. Patterson, setting the dining-room table for our special tea, and encouraging Mrs. Patterson to bake two cakes and an extra large tray of scones. But as the morning passsed, my excitement turned to a stomach-tightening anxiety, mixed with a kind of hopeless depression I had never suffered before. Now wishing only to escape the bustle I had myself created, I crept up to the roof room and sat on the tiny staircase outside the special place where I had once been so untroubled. I examined my innermost feelings. If I told the truth to myself, I didn't want this woman in my life any more than Kate did. I was just being less awkward about it, and trying to make the best of a situation in which my sister let her emotions show honestly. I couldn't hate Helena, because I didn't know her, and I didn't blame Dad for falling in love with someone new; I just wished, with all my heart, that it had never happened. I became very sad, a deep silence growing in me, stilling the nervous excitement of my preparations.

I was sixteen years old and had been more or less happy for as long as I could remember. I had felt lucky to be growing up in the countryside I loved, secure with my father and my sisters and our trips in the car and listening to music and having Alan as an uncomplicated boyfriend and wanting to be an actress and singing and dancing when I felt like it or being absolutely quiet and stretching into life my own way. Now it was all going to end, because of some strange foreign woman, and Dad neglecting us all and agreeing to her plans without a murmur. I wasn't even angry any more, just deeply, quietly, thoroughly upset in the true sense of the word: every thought and emotion thrown about and tumbling to uneasy rest upside-down in the wrong places. I was still sitting sadly on the stairs when a car crunched to a halt on the gravel outside the door and our lives changed for ever.

Room for Love -- Part Two

"Ooh look," squealed Elizabeth as we burst out of the front door, "it's an Austin Mini! Isn't it small?"

I suppose the bright red Mini was a surprise when we were used to Dad's stately grey Wolseley, but I wasn't looking at the car. I was watching my new stepmother having difficulty gettting out of it. I was shocked. She seemed to be all arms and legs. Then, when she had wound herself out of the seat and stepped clear of the door, she stood up and smiled directly at me. She was the tallest woman I had ever seen, and she looked like a film star.

"She's a giantess," whispered Elizabeth, daring to put my exact but unmentionable thought into words.

She was amazingly tall. One hand rested quite naturally on the roof of the car while she waved at us with the other. She seemed to block out the blue light of the sky.

"Hello," she smiled—without whatever accent I had

been expecting.

I was speechless. She was so beautiful. I later learned she was forty-six, yet her face didn't look much older than Kate's; but while my good-looking sister had a sharp nose and lively eyes, Helena's face was round and soft and sweet and girlish—indeed almost babyish—in quite a different way. She was smiling, and her smile made little apples of her cheeks. She had very large lips painted a shocking pale pink I had never seen before, and hugely perfect teeth behind them. Her eyes were her most amazing feature of all. I couldn't help staring right into them, they were so big and blue: pale blue with startling, clear, brilliant whites.

"Hello," she said again, smiling down at us even more broadly. "Isn't it lovely to see you all?"

Somewhere behind all this Dad was opening the tiny boot of the car and saying: "Hello, you two. Where's Kate?" With a large suitcase on one side and Helena on the other, I had never seen him look so small.

Helena's outfit was as extraordinary as her body. She wore a dark purple knitted dress, long-sleeved, but scarcely reaching to her knees. So it was true: they *did* wear shockingly short skirts in London! Her legs were covered in pale-coloured tights and disappeared into white ankle-boots. She was carrying what looked like a white scarf and a long fur coat over one arm, but was still wearing the round fur hat which seemed to go with the coat. The whole effect was of stunning high fashion we had only seen in magazines or films, but with an immaculate, clean-from-the-skin-up, perfectly-groomed finish which was perhaps most impressive of all. Elizabeth and I just looked at each other. We had never imagined anyone so stylish walking into our little country house; even less that they might become one of the family.

Somehow, with everyone talking at once, we all arrived in the front room. Helena threw her coat on to a chair and bent down to kiss us and be properly introduced by Dad. She even kissed Mrs. Patterson on both cheeks like a French hero being given a medal, which left our poor helper even more flustered than she had been already. Then Helena took off her hat, and I noticed she didn't have the very pale blonde hair I had been expecting. It was the colour of dark gold, perhaps going faintly grey in places which gave a streaked look, obviously thick and long, but coiled round her head in a rather severe style which nevertheless suited her perfectly. That was when I became aware of her smell, too. It was a fresh smell, more like a fragrant soap than an actual perfume, although I felt certain she would wear only the most expensive French perfume. I longed to smell like that and be womanly in Helena's gracious but girlish, foreign, glamorous way.

"Well now," she said, revealing at last the trace of an accent, although I would never have guessed it was Swedish, "here we all are."

"All except Kate," said Dad, coming in from the kitchen. "Where the Devil has she got to?"

"She's still at work, Dad," I explained. "You must have raced up the A1."

"We only stopped once," he grinned, "at Grantham. Just keen to get home." He did look boyishly happy, which pleased me greatly. He looked physically fit, too, as if invigorated by a holiday in the sun. "The Mini's quite nippy," he went on, "but rather small for long journeys. Helena likes it for whizzing round London."

He drifted back into the kitchen to ask Mrs. Patterson something. It was as if he had never been away—yet here was this exotic woman who was supposed to be our new mother, sitting with her long legs folded sideways and her knees uncovered and her big pink lips smiling at us. She didn't strike me as being like anyone's stepmother, least of all ours. She was like an enormous sugar-plum fairy, a grown-up Goldilocks, a Hollywood star, a fashion-model, an unbelievably sophisticated elder sister, and something of Brigitte Bardot and a Russian ballerina all rolled into one. She inspired a stunned silence, but it didn't take Elizabeth long to recover her cheek.

"What size shoes do you take?" she asked bluntly, staring at the shockingly modern white boots.

Helena started to laugh. I thought she might rock the settee to pieces if she really let herself go, but out came a soft girlish giggle instead, with little lines appearing round her eyes.

"Seven," she smiled, extending her legs across the room and looking down at her boots. Then she stood up smartly and we ducked mentally in case the ceiling wasn't going to be high enough. "Do you think you'll grow up to be as big as me? You're already very tall for your age." Elizabeth, somewhat abashed under the blue stare, made no answer. "Well, you and Julie have made a lovely tea. Don't you think we had better go and eat it?"

"Would you like to see your room first?" I offered, "Kate is late from work and…"

"No she isn't." Kate's voice broke in as she appeared from the kitchen behind Dad, extending her arm for a rather masculine handshake. "You must be Helena."

Dad laughed loudly and said: "Well she couldn't be anyone else, could she?"

"I can't say how pleased I am to meet you, Darling." Helena put her arms round Kate and kissed her cheeks. "You're just in time for the tea your sisters made for us all. You have very clever sisters."

"Yes, aren't they clever?" replied Kate icily. "It would never have occurred to *me* to make tea."

"Come on you lot," ordered Dad, "and Mrs. Patterson too."

"Och no, I should be away the noo."

"Nonsense, woman. Everyone together for tea. I see you've gone overboard on the scones again. Dish out the jam, Kate. You have no idea how good it feels to be back home with my girls." Dad looked up and suddenly saw himself surrounded by women. "*All* my girls," he added with a laugh.

The meal proceeded, with Dad uncharacteristically doing most of the talking, telling us about the Boat Show and how he had sold his relay instruments at the stand next to the one where Helena had been demonstrating Swedish yachting clothes. I know we all wanted to hear the full story of how they had met and fallen in love, but didn't feel we could ask so soon. Helena—suddenly far less sophisticated than we had imagined her—spent a lot of time looking at Dad with her enormous blue eyes and sharing some private joke in which she would slap him on the leg, giggle with her mouth full, and shuffle her own legs about under the table. He would make sure she had all the food she wanted in easy reach, while she would occasionally wipe his chin then her own mouth with her napkin, smiling and giggling at everything. Had I been only a few years older, I should surely have applauded all this for the lovely display of affection it actually was, but being the age I was, I found it excruciatingly embarrasing. Kate clearly disapproved too, although I guessed her principal emotion would be anger. I took refuge behind my raised teacup. I supposed that Elizabeth, too young for my kind of discomfort, would just think it was 'daft'. Yet at the same time I realised that Dad was happy, and that Helena—shocking though she might be in various ways—had brought an undeniable sparkle of excitement into the house.

The meal was finished, Mrs. Patterson had gone, and we were sitting round the fire in the front room with extra cups of tea, the Winter afternoon darkening beyond the windows. Helena, now less playful, glanced around at the three of us with an odd smile flickering between the pink lips and the blue stare.

"I know a secret," she announced. I thought Elizabeth would burst out with 'Bet you can't keep it then!', but a strange look from Helena ensured we all remained silent. "Yes. You are all ready to hate me."

Before we could say anything to admit or deny it she held up her hand with Dad's new engagement ring on it and silenced us with another queenly gesture.

"I know it is true, and I know you wouldn't be human if you didn't feel this way." Perhaps because this was upsetting her, her accent suddenly seemed stronger. "But it is just that I want you to know I'll do everything I can to make it easy for you to have a new person in the house. I hope you will help me feel at home here, but I want to do things for you also. I want to see you have some fun. I want to help you grow up. Most of all I want to be your friend—if you'll let me."

"Of course we will," I blurted out, almost in tears from her moving speech. "Of course we will!"

"Come on, Darling," said Dad, saving the situation with his usual briskness. "Must show you round. The girls can tidy up," he threw a sharp glance at us, "just this once."

As they went out I heard Helena say quietly: "You were right, James. They really do need a woman."

We cleared up the dishes in silence, knowing that if we started to talk about Helena it would rapidly develop into a loud exchange she would surely overhear. A few minutes later I met my father alone in the hall; Helena obviously still unpacking upstairs. I hugged him long and hard.

"She's lovely, Dad," I whispered. "I'm very very happy for you."

* * *

"Right then," demanded Kate, herding us into the roof room where she had insisted we join her in a council of war. She closed the door firmly. "What are we going to do about the Giantess?"

"Oh Katie," I said, "we don't have to do anything. Let's just be natural." I hated the idea of this conference. It seemed childish and silly and already I was re-aligning my thoughts about Helena and what she might mean to us. "It's just going to be a bit strange at first," I added.

"Strange? I'll say it is," grunted Kate. "I thought Scandinavians were all reserved and chilly. This one's been flinging herself at Dad like a third-rate actress hot for the part."

"They're in love, aren't they?" I felt slightly embarrassed saying it but was determined to make Kate face the truth. "Shouldn't we be happy about that?"

"They can be happy about it if they like," Kate countered sharply, "but we needn't be, not if it's going to make our lives hell."

"Oh honestly, Kate! Why should it? Perhaps we can all get used to this quickly without too much fuss. We should think of Helena too, you know. She must be feeling very strange. We should treat her properly as a guest."

"But that's just it, you little fool," Kate snapped at me. "She's not a guest, she's a wife. She's already conned you into treating her like an exotic visitor here for the holidays—but she's here for good, don't you see? We'll have to put up with her all the time."

I sprang to my feet, annoyed that Kate was treating me like a child and determined to make a stand for what I thought was honesty and fairness.

"You're being rotten, Kate. If you want to know the truth, I liked her straight away and I'm beginning to like her more and more and I don't see why I should deny it or be horrible to her just because you're jealous of her."

"I'm not jealous of her, I just don't like her."

"You *are* jealous, and you're not being very grown-up either. Why can't you just wait and see how things turn out?"

Kate turned on me, her eyes blazing viciously.

"'Cos I know they're going to turn out badly! If you want to suck up to her and be treated like a stupid kid, that's your problem—but *I* won't be. Just take it from me that I'm old enough to know she's a very clever scheming woman, so clever that both of you can't see it."

"And Dad?"

"Dad least of all. So you go on and do what you like with her, but don't expect me to dig you out of the mire when it all goes wrong and she starts using you like she's using Dad."

She stormed out, leaving me with tears in my eyes, and Elizabeth looking at me forlornly. Kate had spoiled this first day right enough; a first day that could have gone really well, just as we might have been starting to come to terms with Helena's new ways. My elder sister, whose help I secretly wanted, had deserted me again.

"Never mind," said Elizabeth with a tenderness which only made me want to cry more. "I like her. I like her a lot, and I think she's going to be fun."

I didn't sense any fun. We all seemed to spend the next few hours keeping out of one another's way, and I don't remember the rest of that evening—apart from Helena coming to kiss me goodnight, her pale lips soft in the darkness, her fragrance the rich scent of a happiness I thought would never be mine.

The events of the next morning, however, are firmly imprinted on my mind. Helena had come down early to breakfast, and must have been at the table before any of us. All the breakfast things were set out neatly, with two pots of tea and a large jug of milk which seemed to have appeared from nowhere, bowls of corn flakes, and more bread and toast and marmalade than we were ever used to. It was all ready on the table, everything together at once. Instead of the usual scramble to and from cupboards which had characterised our breakfasts while Dad had been away, all we had to do was sit down and eat it. Thus, from the very start, Helena had established a régime of brisk and busy mornings, quite unlike Mrs. Patterson's slovenly acceptance that something would have to be done eventually. From the moment I had woken up and automatically begun to get ready for school, I had sensed a new purpose in the house: businesslike, but happy and uncomplicated—provided that everything was done as planned and nobody was lazy or late.

Helena was dressed the part too, in what I guessed were her workaday clothes, but they couldn't have been more unlike our dowdy everyday things. She wore black trousers and flat black shoes, highly polished over brilliant white socks, and a bright red roll-neck jumper which made her face look rounder and younger than ever. Dad appeared, kissed her on the hair, and said she looked like a big robin, which in a way she did. Kate, last to the table, made a great show of indifference to our newly-coloured morning, but even she was wide-eyed when Helena produced our presents.

"I brought you these from London," she explained. "I hope you like them."

Between pouring us all more tea, she planted three transistor radios on the table. They were bright and modern with highly coloured vinyl covers: red-and-cream, blue-and-cream, and black-and-grey. Each had lots of chrome on the front, a big transparent tuning-dial with exciting names and numbers of the radio stations printed under it, and a plastic carrying strap.

"Don't argue about the colours now," she smiled, "although I expect you will."

I had no intention of arguing about the colours.

Mine was the blue-and-cream one and I was delighted with it. Were we all suddenly going to be rich and modern, with exciting things like these coming into the house? The idea of a present from Helena had never entered my mind. Even had I been asked what I might have wanted I should never have thought to say 'a transistor radio', but as soon as I saw it I was thrilled. I knew it would become part of my everyday existence and token of a new kind of life, encapsulating for ever Helena's aura of friendly glamour.

"Well," Dad broke in, "what do you three wretches say?"

"Thank you, of course!" We all seemed to speak at once. "Oh thank you, Helena!"

"When you all come in tonight we'll find the best pop stations," she smiled, showing us her wonderful teeth again. "D'you dance to the latest records, Kate?"

"Not many dances round here," replied Kate dourly, already packing her bag for work. "Must be into Alnwick early today."

"Hey, you've got to show me this famous shop one day," said Helena, "and Alnwick Castle. Don't the Duke and

Duchess live there? I'll give you a lift in the car one morning and we'll have lunch, mmm?"

"'Bye," said Kate, and went for the bus.

"Well now," the big blue eyes turned on Elizabeth, then on me, "school for you two—and no, you can't take your radios, but we'll get them going tonight, I promise."

I was still in a dream, amazed that such things should be happening, but Elizabeth had recovered her usual inquisitive self.

"What are you going to do today?" she asked Helena.

"Oh, I'm still unpacking my clothes and helping your father re-arrange things in our bedroom."

I was still intrigued and distracted by the sound of her voice, and had to keep reminding myself that it was Dad more than any of us who was at the very middle of this exciting upheaval.

"D'you say 'Dad' in Sweden, or is it always 'Father'?" persisted Elizabeth.

"Sometimes we say 'Papa'," answered Helena.

"You're not going to start calling me 'Papa'," Dad grimaced aimiably to his new wife.

"Don't worry," she replied evenly, "I'll keep calling you 'James'—for a few years, anyway."

This little piece of adult banter was lost on Elizabeth, but I detected its loving jokiness: something else which had never existed in the house before.

* * *

The radios were a great success, and the first weeks of Helena's presence swung to the new beat of pop music. The novelty of this in some way detracted from her own, yet at the same time accompanied her movement into our lives. Even without hindsight, I realised I was hearing something new and special and that there could scarcely have been a better time to open our ears to it. 1964: there was so much! I especially remember The Dave Clark Five beating away with *Glad All Over* and Cilla Black's soulful *Anyone Who Had a*

Heart, but of course it was The Beatles who perfectly embodied the spirit of the times and who seemed to sing exactly what I was thinking—but to music nobody else could have created. I quickly became an avid Beatles fan. I think Dad looked somewhat askance at my rapt attention to the radio and my desperate attempts to save up for a record-player, but I had always been deeply and strangely moved by music—and it was the pure music, rather than the associated excitements of fashion and style, which really stirred me. I knew the world was in the grip of something new: this was the irresistible sound of it. I also knew it was the music of my own time and my own age, loud and sweet, and that nobody could take that magic away from me. I was delighted when I saw Helena's own record-player arrive from London in the next van-load of her possessions…and absolutely thrilled when she smilingly handed it over to me. The money I had saved went on Beatles LPs.

Helena herself liked pop music, and she would often tap her feet and sway her body to whichever radio had been left in the kitchen; but her true tastes in music, like her true character, were deeper and darker and softer and sweeter. With her record-player came a small but impressive record collection. There was a wonderful album of Strauss waltzes, which I remember Kate tossed aside as 'desperately old-fashioned' but which I clung to, neatly demonstrating the differences between my elder sister and myself. Helena loved the waltzes too, and would swing her arms to the beat, although I never saw her carried away into the dances which whirled through my imagination. My favourite was *Roses from the South* with its long lilting phrase seeming to slide itself under my very heartstrings. It stirred all kinds of images of Helena and myself in romantic ballgowns, of sunsets over forested hills, castles by a dark river, soldiers, medals, gardens, palaces, and pink and golden clouds. But it was music of another Strauss which most powerfully illustrated my relationship with the serene yet girlish woman who seemed more like a grown-up friend than a stepmother. When she first played her record of Richard Strauss's *Der Rosenkavalier* I thought it strange and difficult music, but very soon I was enraptured by its passages of haunting beauty, its grand waltz, its soulful romance. I played it in the dark evenings, the house still tangy with the Winter smoke of our coal fires. I played it on bright Saturday mornings, Dad taking Elizabeth out to help him with the shopping. As the Spring began, it became the music of all my hopes and anxieties and nameless yearnings.

* * *

It was announced that Helena was to keep her flat in London, at least for the foreseeable future, and maintain her involvement with the Swedish firm of sportswear manufacturers whose yachting products she had promoted at the Boat Show. Every so often she would spend a few days in London and the house seemed truly dull without her; then she would return with more luggage and clothes. As the weather improved she took to wearing short skirts and knee-socks, always with immaculately polished shoes and perfectly groomed hair. We had never seen a woman dress in this way, and although I felt I might never wear them with such style, I longed to have clothes like Helena's. Yet while we were full of admiration, envy, or just surprise, we discovered she had definite plans for the three plainly dressed girls in her new family.

"I've been meaning to ask you all," said Helena over one of our neatly organised breakfasts, "wouldn't you like some new clothes?"

I wasn't sure what answer she was expecting, but it couldn't have been Elizabeth's blunt: "We always wear these things." The announcement was made with a defiant pride in her own dowdiness.

"Yes I know, Darling," replied Helena pointedly, "that's why I thought you would like something new. We could go to the shops in Newcastle. I understand there are lots of good shops, but of course I haven't been. You could show me. They're sure to have some wonderful new things."

I guessed this was her nice way of telling us we were terribly old-fashioned, but Kate wasn't having it.

"We never go anywhere to wear them," she stated flatly.

"Well I think that will change, Kate," Helena smiled mysteriously. "You must come down to London with me some time; then of course we may have some parties."

"What, in this house?" cried Kate. "Entertain people, here?"

"Yes. Why not?"

"Dad's never had people here," continued Kate. "It's too out of the way."

"No it isn't. People have cars, you know. Anyway, *you* like parties, don't you, Elizabeth?"

"I like Birthday parties," replied Elizabeth with her mouth full, "as long as there are cakes and things."

"Then we will have a Birthday party. Whose Birthday is it next?"

"Mine," grunted Kate, leaving the table. "April the Fourth."

"She sounds like a queen," sneered Elizabeth without looking at her. "April the Fourth: the queen who came after April the Third, the bad one with the hump." Kate glared back. "But we never dress up for anything," continued Elizabeth, "we hate dressing up."

Helena looked desperately around the table, and I felt acutely sorry for her.

"I like dressing up," I stated firmly.

"No you don't," argued Elizabeth.

"Yes I do!" I shouted, almost in tears, though whether for Helena's sake or my own, I couldn't tell. "I love dressing up! I'd love a new dress as well: a proper dress, and go to parties in it, and spend lots of time getting ready, and wear make-up and a necklace and everything."

The others fell silent at my outburst. I loved Helena for her kindness and for possessing the maturity I so much wanted—but I couldn't say so and went red while she smiled at me.

"We'll see what we can do," she said. "I have another idea, too," she continued to everyone. I could not tell if she was undaunted by the hostile responses she had suffered from Kate and Elizabeth, encouraged by my passionate confession, or just plunging on with her own ideas for improving us all. "I think it would be very good if we could convert the loft into a proper room. It would be perfect for parties and dancing."

Kate exploded.

"What? The roof room?" she cried.

"Yes, that's what you call it, isn't it? The roof room."

"But that's *our* room! We do all sorts of things in

there. We've put our plays on in there. No, it's a horrible idea…"

She ranted on, completely destroying the uneasy settlement we had just managed to create around the table. My heart sank. While Kate was furious, I felt only a dull sadness. I didn't want the roof room converted into anything new; it was the storehouse of so many happy memories. Yet at the same time, I admired Helena and had become so excited by everything she represented that I never wanted to hurt or insult her as Kate was doing. Suddenly, I just wanted none of this to have happened. I wanted to be back on a darkening afternoon in the Christmas holidays with the tea things cleared away, Dad dozing at the fire, and a rehearsal going on in the roof room. I didn't hate Helena with Kate's vehemence, but for a moment I wished Dad had never met her. Then, in an instant, looking at Helena's blue eyes, I realised I was wrong. The roof room *should* be converted; we *should* move forward, all of us, into whatever new life Helena was bringing. It was fresh and new and the natural way we were going. Above all it was loving, and we had been starved of love. We should take it, take it all, and not hate Helena but love her in return.

"No, Kate," I found myself speaking quite calmly,

"don't be like that. I think we *should* convert the roof room. It would be excellent for parties. We don't do plays up there any more."

"You," she snorted, "you! You're the one who wants to be an actress and you're giving our theatre away."

"I didn't know you wanted to be an actress, Darling," Helena smiled at me, trying to rise above the harsh words spoken around her. "Nobody told me that. You get big parts in the school plays, do you?"

"No, actually I don't, but I do want to be an actress," I reddened again as I admitted it, "but not just in the school play or in the roof room. I want to learn to be a proper actress at drama school and go into films—but not in the roof room any more. We've done all that—don't you see, Kate? Let's have parties up there instead." I had amazed myself with my own honesty and was incapable of saying anything else.

"Well," Helena was speaking again, "that's something new to think about; it's a lot to think about. Please, we must not argue about it any more. We must decide sensibly, then we'll do what we all agree is best. It's just an idea—about the roof room, I mean. What a wonderful idea about you being an actress, Julie. You must tell me more about it."

It took a long time before I could bring myself to speak openly about my once-secret ambition, but I knew now that Helena—of all people—was the one who should be told. We did talk about it, and forged a new friendship.

Helena was making soup, striding purposefully about the kitchen with cups full of lentils and barley then standing pensively over her steaming pan.

"You could play Juliet: you've got the right name for it. You could say those great words from the balcony." She stirred the soup and looked up at the ceiling. "You know: 'A rose by any other name would smell as sweet.'"

"You make it sound marvellous," I said, awed by the intensity and naturalism she put into the well-known quotation.

"Not me—it's Mister Shakespeare. Anyway, you'd make a much better Juliet. I'd never pass myself off as a beautiful young Italian girl. Look at me. They'd have to shrink me and paint me brown."

We laughed at the outrageous idea of it.

"But seriously," I went on, "I wouldn't want to go through all Juliet goes through and then die at the end. No thanks."

"Well, let me see now," she looked me up and down. "You could be Beatrice in *Much Ado About Nothing*."

"Oh, no!" I squealed. "Argue all the time? She's horrible! We're doing that play at school. They're supposed to be in love, but they spend the whole script fighting. That's not my idea of being in love. Beatrice is a part for Kate," I declared wickedly, "and we won't say anything about who should star in *The Taming of the Shrew*."

"Oh you girls!" Helena shook her wooden spoon at me. "You should be more tolerant of one another."

"We try to be."

"I know *you* try."

"So I'd have to play Hero in *Much Ado*. I am more like her."

"Well, yes, that's good casting. I seem to remember

she gets a good husband in the end too, perhaps the best one."

"She does, but I agree Beatrice is the best female part, even if she and Benedick do argue when they're supposed to be in love."

"Don't they argue *because* they're in love?"

"Perhaps. Someone in the play does say they have a 'merry war'."

"Well, you could put that in one of your essays at school and amaze your teachers."

"I just might," I grinned.

"I have my uses, you see."

"Honestly, Helena, I just never imagined having this kind of talk with you. Never. It's wonderful. *You* are wonderful."

"Now you will embarrass me." She stirred the soup. "It's interesting we should be talking about these things now. I saw *Much Ado* on the big stage at Stratford two Summers ago. It's a lovely play. I also studied Shakespeare when I was at school, you know."

"Really? Shakespeare in Sweden?"

"Oh yes. Of course as you probably know there have been great dramatists in Scandinavia, but none of them are as much fun as William Shakespeare. I like the plays; I studied them a lot. It's lucky I didn't end up speaking Seventeenth-Century English."

"Your English is brilliant," I said in true admiration of her fluency. "I just know I could never learn Swedish so well."

"No," she grinned. "Learn acting instead, eh? Of course you'd have to go to Drama School, show some talent, and work hard—but from what I hear you could do that all right."

"I'm not so sure. I think I'm better at telling other people how to act than acting myself."

"A director then."

"Yes, I'd really like to do that."

"That would be good; not many women directors. I

think you'd still have to go to Drama School first and at least try some acting. I took acting lessons, you know, when I was starting out as a model. It was fun."

"You're a model?"

"Yes of course, that was my job. I thought you knew."

"I knew you were modelling yachting clothes at Earls Court."

"Ah yes," she laughed. "I'm sure you've all been told that story. It really wasn't so glamorous, you know. Those waterproofs and rubber hats were not very nice under the hot lights, and the deck shoes were not comfortable. I would always prefer not to wear shoes on a boat. Still," she grinned, striking a pose with her spoon, "one yachtsman liked the way I looked, and all my hard work had a happy ending, eh?"

"But a real fashion model," I went on. "How exciting, with photographers and everything, and having your picture in the magazines! I'd love to see your magazine pictures—you must look so beautiful. You *are* so beautiful," I added shyly, looking away from her. "I just wanted to tell you that," I hurried on, gaining confidence in my confession.

"I suppose everyone tells you that, I suppose Dad tells you that, but I just wanted to say it myself, to let you know I think you're the most beautiful person I've ever seen, the most beautiful woman in the world…and not just to look at. You're a good and kind and beautiful person *inside*."

Was there the tiny twinkle of a tear in her eye, a flush of embarrassment across her friendly smile, looking down at me with such kindness?

"I am glad you think so, Julie," she said quietly, then chuckled and stirred the soup again. "But I do assure you, I am *not* the most beautiful woman in the world. Isn't that Sophia Loren? Well, anyway, God puts people together in different ways, and some people are lucky with the arrangement of their bits and pieces—but it's inside that matters, you know."

"I do know. That's what I'm saying. That's why I wanted to tell you. We all thought you might not be so nice, you know."

I was left a little shaky after my admission; Helena seemed to shrug it off with a laugh.

"I was the Wicked Witch of the Northlands, was I?

Come to steal your father away? Well, that was a perfectly natural thing to be worried about—and very honest of you to tell me. I admire that. But I haven't been *that* bad, have I?"

"No, of course not", I laughed as she defused the situation with an overdone grimace. "And I still think you're the most beautiful person on the *outside*. I just wanted to say it, even though everyone else does as well."

"Actually, *not* everyone says it, my Darling—so thank you."

There was a pause in our conversation as she moved around the kitchen, finding dried herbs to put in the soup. I had never felt closer to her, nor less shy about being myself.

"Yes," she was saying again, "modelling is fun, but acting is much more difficult, and really a much better and more important thing to do. I'd love to help you do it, Julie."

"That would be great!"

"I don't know I could help you get in to Drama School," she went on, "but I do know some agents in London. I'll call them and find out more for you. They could be a good contact when you get down there. It never hurts to know the right people."

"That's one of Dad's sayings."

"I know," she said severely. "It's terrible. I'm turning more like him every day."

We burst out laughing together...and that laugh dissolved into the smiles of our new acceptance, understanding, and love.

* * *

It was eventually decided that the conversion should go ahead. When the roof room had been cleared out it looked larger than we had ever imagined. A joiner came to fit a new and bigger window frame where the tiny skylight had been and to replace the ancient floorboards with clean, fresh-smelling planks of pine. Now there was a big new space in the house waiting to be filled. The excitement of this cancelled out any sadness I might have felt as the old curtain-rail and lights came down and our theatre in the roof effectively disappeared; but I know it still rankled with Kate.

She refused to have anything to do with the work as it progressed.

Helena put up modern light-fittings and varnished the woodwork. Dad, completely and boyishly absorbed, went shopping for nails and sandpaper. He scampered—that was the only word for it—up and down the stairs while his wife worked steadily at the top of the house: golden-haired queen-captain steering us into our new life.

"She *is* making it like a ship," remarked the perceptive Elizabeth, who had become Helena's most energetic week-end helper. It was true: our dusty, dirty playroom and junk-store was beginning to look like the cabin of a large yacht. Were we in the Baltic, with white sails hoisted somewhere above the rafters? With brass fittings in the room and the blue Northern light flooding in through its sparkling new window, the illusion was almost complete. Helena tied her hair back in a thick ponytail and worked in a faded blue jersey and rolled-up jeans; bare arms catching the sunlight, bare feet stroking the pale wood. I noticed her skin was the same colour as the clean blonde pine, as if she had somehow grown naturally out of the same forest. Swinging up into the rafters, gripping the beams with her toes and clenching a screwdriver between her teeth, she was a very different Helena from the sophisticated businesswoman we had first met. I began to sense other reasons why Dad had fallen so completely under her spell, why Kate was so furious, and why I could never share her anger. I also began to understand how Helena was irresistable to men, which—if Kate saw it all—would surely serve to increase my sister's detestation. It stirred only greater admiration in me. Helena was good at everything, yet simple and unaffected, never pushy or conceited. She was clever and capable without being threatening. She was always beautiful and utterly feminine: as desirable with a paintbrush in our roof room as with a cocktail glass at a London party, perhaps more desirable than ever to Dad now she was the barefoot yachting girl with sea-blue eyes and sun-golden hair, rigging the house for a new and happy voyage to a paradise just teasingly over the horizon. So how could any man fail to love her; how could any woman fail to understand; and why could Kate not accept her with the same enjoyment as my own?

One day I made the terrible mistake of saying something like this to Kate. She turned on me with a shocking fury.

"I'm just about sick of you!" She grabbed my wrist

and shouted into my face. "She's got you, hasn't she? You and Elizabeth. She's not content with Dad; she's had to make you two as daft as he is!"

"What do you mean?" I cried.

"You know what I mean: all dewy-eyed just because she paints her nails and dresses up like a barmaid. The way you look at her when she walks into a room you'd think she was the Queen of bloody Sheba!"

"But Dad couldn't help falling in love with her," I protested. "He was *right* to fall in love with her!"

"And you know all about love, do you, you little idiot?"

"I know it when I see it."

"And this is it, is it? Simpering about the house, oohing and aahing at a bit of blonde hair any fool could get out of a bottle, stuffing yourselves with her fancy cakes, listening to foreign fairy-stories? You make me sick!"

For a moment I thought she was going to hit me. I felt frightened, but worse than that, I felt dirty and disgusted. There had never been swearing or violence in this house. We didn't know about these things, didn't want to, didn't need to. Now Kate was thrusting them into my face. Kate had done this, my own sister; she was to blame. I felt a horrible anger too, as if suddenly infected by hers. I discovered—despite what some people would have had me believe—that bad things could not always be put right, vile knowledge unlearned, and hurtful words cancelled out. Once they were there, they had done their evil work. I struggled in Kate's grip. Again I thought she was going to hit me...but she didn't, she just tore her hand away, hurting me as she pulled my wrist.

"I *do* know about love!" I screamed. "And who's going to love you anyway, when you're so nasty to everybody?"

Kate walked away.

"I'll put an end to all this," she said coldly, without looking back at me. "I'll show you. I'll show you all."

Room for Love -- Part Three

I was horrified to think what Kate might do, but dare not confess my anxieties to anyone. She appeared to do nothing. She still went about sullen and short-tempered, but she did swallow her fury and allow herself to be taken on the much-anticipated 'Great Shopping Trip to Newcastle'.

It might have been easier, although probably less fun, to fit the four of us into Dad's big Wolseley, but Elizabeth had persistently begged a ride in Helena's Mini, and this was to be it. Dressed as smartly as we could be in our Winter coats, Elizabeth and I squeezed into the narrow back seat.

"Kate had better sit in the front," said Helena. "Make sure you've all got your handbags."

"I don't have a handbag," stated Elizabeth.

"Well, make sure your money is in your inside pocket."

We settled ourselves and waved a noisy goodbye to Dad. With Helena looking more like a giantess than ever with her knees behind the steering-wheel, we zoomed down the Great North Road and were soon looking for a parking space off Northumberland Street, in those days the main shopping centre of Newcastle.

It was a cold morning with an open blue sky and seagulls yelping between the tall buildings. Newcastle had never seemed more exciting to me: here we were with the glamorous Helena locking up her trendy little car and patting it on the roof. We tried to keep up with her long stride down the busy pavements. Kate and she seemed to have buried the difficulties between them, at least for today, and were indulging in what I thought was very grown-up talk about clothes. Elizabeth chattered furiously, pointing out cars and policemen and curious displays in shop windows. As usual, I was the quiet one, but even if I had wanted to speak, I could not have found words to express myself that morning. Yet amongst every other emotion of excitement, I knew one thing: I felt rich in Helena's company. I had saved a few pounds for this trip and had them in my purse ready to spend if I saw something which took my fancy, but Helena was going to spend much more on each of us. Somehow it had never been the done thing to talk about money with

Dad: we must have been quite poor and only just managed to run our simple lives. I never thought to ask how. In almost shocking contrast, Helena had openly said she had plenty of money and was going to use it to buy us the new clothes she wanted us to have. So here we were, swaggering into the best shops in Newcastle and hoping to come out looking like fashion-models. That's what I hoped anyway. I could never be absolutely sure what my sisters were thinking when Helena was there.

"Coffee first, I think," she smiled, leading us into Fenwick's.

"But you don't know they have a café in here," protested Elizabeth awkwardly.

"Oh yes they do. James told me." How grown-up it made me feel that she had called him 'James' and not 'your father'. "And he said it's the best dress shop in Newcastle—but what does he know, eh girls?" We giggled at her naughty blue-eyed smile. "We'll try C&A just across the street there then we'll go anywhere we like. But definitely coffee first. Come on."

She led us into Fenwick's. Of course I had been inside the big store a few times before, but it had never seemed more intriguing. Were the shoppers really so wealthy, were the assistants really so elegant and perfectly groomed as they stood beside their counters and their rails of dresses? Had there ever been such an array of expensive perfume, such gleaming crystal, such multi-coloured kitchenware?

"That reminds me," remarked Helena, "I must have some new pans. We'll come back for those another day…Oh look, there's the delicatessen. I'm sure they won't have any Swedish sausage, but shall we see?"

They did not have any Swedish sausage, so she bought some Polish sausage instead.

"It's delicious," she told us. "Just wait 'til I cook it for you tonight. We'll have some salami and some paté, too."

I had never eaten or even seen food like this before, and felt very exotic just carrying it.

We sat down in the café and Helena bought us coffee and biscuits. Then we made for the fashion department, where our lives changed yet again. Within an hour Helena had bought a very expensive matching skirt and jacket for Kate, who looked lovely when she came out of the fitting-room, even if her rather tired and inescapably 'sensible' brown shoes didn't go with the new red and grey outfit.

"It needs a hat," mused Helena.

"A little round hat," I suggested.

"Like an air-hostess," put in Elizabeth.

So a little round hat was bought, and later a pair of ankle-boots, the like of which we'd never seen in the family, except of course on Helena. Elizabeth emerged grinning madly in a blue and white geometrically patterned mini-dress with tight sleeves and a high neck.

"She looks like Cilla Black!" exclaimed Kate.

"Oh no," I said, "like a girl in a French film." Of course I hadn't seen any French films, but it seemed an exciting thing to say.

I think I got the best outfit: a truly elegant cream-coloured trouser-suit with tiny slits at the ankles, three-quarter-length sleeves, and two outsized buttons on the front.

"Very smart," said Kate.

"Very modern," said Elizabeth.

"Very sexy," said Helena—and for the first time in my life, I felt it.

We didn't need further excitement after that, but Helena insisted on providing more. We went round the other big shops, bought Elizabeth a blue handbag, and returned to Fenwick's for lunch in the stylish restaurant there. With our own money we bought sweets and make-up and I found a headband which I thought would go really well with my trouser-suit. Eventually we squeezed back into the tiny car, which seemed smaller than ever now that we had so many bags and boxes. We arrived home in the early dusk and tumbled into the house, opening parcels and laughing and trying on one another's clothes while Helena cooked the Polish sausage and served up the paté with hot brown bread. The atmosphere was as magical as an unexpected Christmas morning.

* * *

So, despite her threats, it looked as if Kate was unable to change the impression that Helena was too good to be true. She was beautiful, talented, kind, generous, lovable, and exciting; but she was still a stranger—until the day we went to Holy Island.

Every year, Dad and the three of us would make at least one visit to Lindisfarne. The unique atmosphere of Holy Island, the business of crossing the causeway at low tide, the ancient priory, the spectacular views over dramatic mud-flats, the mysterious coastline, the feeling of being on an island which was not always an island: all these fascinated us. We were each affected in different ways, although I think Dad was perhaps most moved by the place, and we knew we had to take Helena, for his pleasure and for ours. It would be like showing her a secret and precious possession. I felt, with a curious sense of inevitability, that to share it with her would be to finally accept her—and I wanted to finally accept her. I hoped desperately that she would enjoy the visit, feel the same emotions the island stirred in me, and remember this day all her life.

A week-end came in early Spring when the tides were convenient for a morning crossing and the weather seemed to be holding fair for a few days, so we decided to go on the Sunday. Kate backed out of the arrangement saying she and Richard had a date she couldn't break. Helena looked disappointed, but I was not truly sorry to be going without Kate. Her sourness would not match my dreams of the place, nor my hopes for an untroubled day.

The jaunty rhythm of Strauss's *Tritsch Tratsch Polka* danced in my head as we packed the Wolseley with wellingtons, coats, binoculars, walking-sticks, and the large picnic which Helena had spent much time preparing on the Saturday evening. The music was still running through me as Dad drove on to the damp causeway, the receding tide glistening away to the South under cloudless sunshine. The polka did not go with this wild scenery, and I changed my in-head version of it to Eric Coates's *Elizabeth of Glamis*, which was also in Helena's record collection. The haunting Scots atmosphere of that music stirred my soul as we parked the car near the harbour and went for a walk around the island.

We set off through the narrow streets of the village; craned our necks to look at the red sandstone 'rainbow arch' bridging the sky in the ruined priory; watched gulls scream over the shallow lake in the middle of the island; came to the bleak dunes on its North shore; looked for seals on the black rocks but saw none; admired the magnificent views beyond

Berwick right up to Scotland and back to the Cheviot Hills; walked beneath the dramatic castle on Beblowe Crag; and gave ourselves up to the quiet magic of the island, bathed in mild Spring sunshine and encircled by the hiss of the sea as it worked its serenity into our souls. We felt, without being able to say exactly why, that we were part of something unchanging and timeless, and that we were free to wander within a realistic, reachable, everyday kind of paradise.

"This is wonderful," Helena kept saying, putting her hands in the pockets of her coat and drinking in the views. She strolled softly between Dad and myself, Elizabeth skipping about and picking up stones. The island had put her in reflective mood, quite unlike her more usual brightly-smiling brisk and efficient self.

"Spring can be like this in Sweden," she observed, looking out to sea from underneath the castle crag, "mild and still...and do you hear the birds?" We watched a lark singing joyously as it climbed into the magnificent blue. "That one is somehow very English. Of course in Sweden there's no mistaking the Seasons: it's properly hot in Summer and terribly cold in Winter with the snow piled up everywhere. And Spring and Autumn are as they should be: somewhere in between; just like this, in fact."

"D'you get homesick for Sweden?" I asked her.

"No, I'm just remembering it."

"D'you get homesick for London?" asked Elizabeth.

"No, I never get homesick for London. It's fun but it's not home. No, I was happy in Sweden, but I'm happier here, now, with all of you. I love all of you."

This, I thought, is the woman we were all so ready to hate, and she loved all of us. I felt ashamed at having once been so determined to dislike her, but grateful that I had suddenly grown up enough to understand and have her as a wonderful friend. Of course it was Elizabeth who went to the painful crux of the matter.

"Do you love Kate as much as you love us? After all, *she* wouldn't come on this outing. She's always saying she hates you, anyway."

Helena took Elizabeth's hand and my hand together at the same time—just like a real mother, I thought with the beginnings of tears in my eyes. She bent down to us, not only because she was so tall, but I think because she wanted to love us and cuddle us and tell us the truth about herself.

Dad was somewhere near, but he had decided to say nothing in the kind of situation where many another father might have disciplined Elizabeth. I couldn't look at him to check how he was taking it; I could only look up into those bright blue eyes with their little lines of age and sorrow wrinkling at the corners. How hurt she must have been.

"I don't think Kate really hates me, Darling. The truth is she resents me. D'you know what that word means?"

"Not really." Elizabeth hung her head in her own kind of stubborn shame at having said something so unsettling, and her own kind of anger at having allowed herself to be caught saying it. A lesser woman than Helena might have been very harsh with her.

"It means she thinks I'm going to take everything away from her: everything she cares about, like you and your Dad and Julie, and the house where she's grown up, and all the things she's done and enjoyed for so long—but I'm not. You see that, don't you? I'm not going to take anything away from any of you. I just want to *give* you things; give you everything, give you and your Dad all the love I've got. I have been lonely too, you know: all those years working in London, my family dead or far away. Will you love me,

Elizabeth—and you, Julie? I want you to love me…oh, I want you to love me…not just because I buy you presents but because you think I'm good and worthy of your love. That's what I really want. Kate knows that, I know she does, she's just growing up, that's all, just wanting to let us all know she can be her own woman. You'll love me, won't you? That's what I really want."

She was on her knees in the damp grass, hugging us close to her, so we could see nothing but the texture of her coat, smell her perfumed hair, and taste our own tears mixed with hers. We were shocked. This was beside the castle on Holy Island, where we had come every year since we were little, with visitors strolling past and having picnics in their cars. This sort of thing just didn't happen here, to people like us. Yet here we were, inescapably on view, with the place we knew and the people we had been utterly transformed, crying into the shoulders of this tall Swedish woman who suddenly really was our new mother baring her soul to us and crying back down on to our hair: the new mother whom we loved, at that moment, more than anyone or anything else.

Hours later, as I was washing my face before going to bed at the end of our long day out, I overheard Dad talking to Helena. I heard him say, with a tenderness that brought me near to tears again, "Just say the same things to Kate, will you, my love?" And I said to myself, as I dried my face: "We're a real family now, however Kate takes it."

* * *

I am sure Helena did say those things to Kate, but I couldn't tell what effect they had. Events rushed on. Mrs. Patterson left us, quite amicably, since the running of the house and all the cooking was now under Helena's more than capable control. The conversion of the roof room neared completion. Dad seemed cheerily happy. Elizabeth, already tall for her age, grew even taller and certainly put on weight as a result of Helena's meaty dinners and pastry-piled teas. Kate spent less time with us and more with Richard. I suppose I was just coming to realise that the clash between Kate and Helena was not only inevitable, but incurable: two women in the same kitchen, so to speak. But Kate made the impasse needlessly cruel. She knew, like all of us now, that Helena really wanted to make the new family work and would have done so sweetly, beautifully, brilliantly and without upset...if only Kate had allowed it. My elder sister did not possess the grace to help her, but she did have the intelligence to realise that the battle she had made was lost. Once she saw that Helena was here to stay and that the rest of us loved her, all she really wanted was to get out with as little discussion as possible...but even Kate, noticeably short on words these days, had to explain how she would be leaving.

"Richard's asked me to marry him," she declared one evening.

So, was this how she was going to 'show us all'? Not very original, not even very nasty, but very convenient. Did we all sound just a little too delighted when we heard she had accepted?

Of course this provoked yet more family upheaval: weeks of chatter and planning, and another dose of that unsettling feeling that things could never be the same again, but there was fun in it, too. Elizabeth and I looked at Richard with new eyes and teased him in new ways when he called to formally ask Dad's permission to marry Kate. We were going to be bridesmaids, and Helena was actually going to make our dresses. Up in the roof room, barefoot again in her rolled-up jeans, she went about on her hands and knees, cutting out yards of lilac satin. Even Elizabeth allowed herself to become obsessed with clothes for this event as our hearts beat faster to the exciting swishes of dress fittings and the whispers of new soft shoes across the freshly varnished boards.

In the middle of all this I felt a great peace come over me and over the family. Kate was leaving us. I should have been sad but I wasn't. Already her absence on long nights out with Richard allowed me to relax into what I sensed was to be the new shape of the family, at least for the foreseeable future. Elizabeth was growing into it, too. Dad, Helena, and the two of us would sit round the fire, snuggling into chairs or on the floor, warm against the cold March evenings, talking as we had never talked before.

"You're always so wonderfully clean," said Elizabeth to Helena, admiring her dazzling pink jumper and long white socks; this from the girl who went about, as Dad put it, 'with mud up to her eyes'.

"And you've done a wonderful job in the roof room," I added, "that's like you too: all clean and bright."

"You'll have me like a washing-powder advert," laughed Helena. "Now you know it's just the way I like to be. Life can be so full of unpleasant things outside; but inside, with our own persons, we can be clean and careful and celebrate life in little things like clothes and houses. They are important things though, if they make us happy and let us be content. Do you understand?"

"I think so," answered Elizabeth, plunging along from images of clean socks and nicely painted windows to a philosophy of sensuality and the meaning of life.

"Yes, of course you understand," smiled Helena, "or you wouldn't have made the flag in the soap for me. That was a lovely thing to see in my new home."

"Love cannot exist without a little innocence," Dad put in unexpectedly. "Albert Camus."

"Who?"

"Albert Camus: a French writer, and a good one. He said 'Love cannot exist without a little innocence'…meaning, I suppose, that to fully experience the happiness of love we need to celebrate the little innocent things, instead of just grabbing lustfully at each other." He made big eyes at us. "Which reminds me, I hope Richard isn't grabbing lustfully at Kate…well, not too lustfully."

We giggled at the thought of it.

"Kate is quite capable of taking care of herself and fighting off the men," smiled Helena, "especially Richard."

We laughed aloud.

"The poor boy is…what's that English expression of yours, James?"

"Putty in her hands. But he'll toughen up when he has to run the marriage."

"What do you mean, run the marriage, you old-fashioned thing?" Helena shook Dad's knee playfully as he sat on the arm of her chair. "They'll run it together, equally. That's how it's done these days, or hadn't you noticed?"

"You mean Kate will give the orders!" squealed Elizabeth. "Anyway, *women* always run a marriage—that's what Mrs. Liddell says at school."

"Wise woman," winked Dad.

"A Biology teacher should know better than to say such things," stated Helena. "Oh well, as long as they talk; that's what matters, from day one. They'll have to talk out what they want to do, how they want to live."

"What did you and Helena talk about when *you* first met?" Elizabeth shuffled closer to Dad.

"Oh, all sorts of things. Work, of course—but not too much about work. Helena's life in Sweden; ours here in England."

"But didn't you want to know all about each other before you proposed? Didn't you ask each other all sorts of questions?"

"Yes," answered Helena, "but not too many questions; it's rather rude to bombard someone you've just met with a lot of questions. We just got to know each other perfectly naturally, at the right pace."

"It sounds like you moved pretty quickly to me, Dad," I observed to general giggles.

How good it felt to be able to talk like this to Dad and Helena as they sat together, to say these things right in front of them, without feeling embarrassed or silly.

"But you must have asked her *something*," persisted Elizabeth, "if only to start the conversation. Surely you didn't just stare at each other."

Now we did feel embarrassed and silly, but only for a moment. Dad put an arm round Helena and grinned at Elizabeth.

"Oh yes," said Helena, "there was quite a lot of staring."

"Actually," Dad looked at her, "I did ask a very important question, didn't I?" He turned back to Elizabeth. "But I think that was after I proposed."

"Well?" Elizabeth was goggle-eyed.

"I said 'Is there anywhere you especially like to be kissed?'"

We giggled ferociously behind our knees, but we felt marvellously grown-up at the same time. It was Helena herself, with an extra wide-eyed smile, who gave us the answer we were burning to know.

"Back of the neck, actually."

More giggles, and a somewhat abashed Elizabeth.

"It was very sexy and romantic," continued Helena, pouring more coffee. "I hope some young men ask you the same question some day—and that you give the poor boys a chance to show you how lovely loving can be."

"And don't giggle in their faces either," said Dad.

"If you say so, Dad."

Of course we giggled even more, but we loved him even more, and Helena too, and thought ourselves very special and adult that we should come to know such things. And because it had ended so swiftly with Helena's dramatic arrival, only now did I realise we had suffered a terrible loneliness: a loneliness akin to poverty, an inability to share and enjoy things we had no real wish to have kept locked up in ourselves for ever. Now we were rich, now we were free. What we used to say to one another had been a kind of silence; now we could speak out and be heard—by someone new, and by one another.

We accepted, too, that the loneliest of all had been Dad. His long-suffering self-sufficiency, his dutiful bringing-up of three daughters, his dedicated inventiveness and the development of his business, all had been toil in a long, long drought. Now the rivers of his soul had flooded again. Bright and golden, Helena had spun him round and woven our world together. So now all joys might be celebrated in a kind of universal language: from delight in a prettily set tea-table and neatly groomed hair to an appreciation of love and humanity. Suddenly, we could all be in love with life and be blessed with the richness to live it and the freedom to say so; to be innocent, not having to be clever, and so inherit the love of which Camus had written—not that we'd read or even heard of Camus before, but we reckoned he was a great man for having Dad quote him, and for suddenly meaning something to us. Though death and dullards might stalk the Earth, we could fling sand in their faces and make merry. It was a wonderful lesson to have learned as we sat in our cosy front room, sailing safely through the chilly night into our new lives.

* * *

Helena pronounced the roof room completed, and we all trooped up to inspect her handiwork. The place had been transformed into a cool, blonde, open, wooden room with shiny floorboards. A long bar-counter from which to serve food and drinks ran down one side; there was a special place for the record-player, a big modern settee covered in yellow fabric, and a mound of brightly-coloured cushions in one corner. It was a place for fun and parties, a fantasy made real—her fantasy, not ours—yet all the more attractive for being so out-of-keeping with the rest of the house. She said we should 'christen' the room with a big party for Kate's Birthday on April the Fourth.

And we did. The night before Kate's Birthday, Helena introduced us to the Swedish custom of the Birthday Breakfast Tray. Late at night, the biggest tray we had in the house was covered with a special cloth. In the middle went a joint present from Dad and Helena: a very large and expensive box of make-up. Helena had wrapped it in shiny pink paper with the kind of oversized satin bow we had only seen in Hollywood musicals. On top of this went a precarious arrangement of the breakfast things and around it our own presents to Kate, clustering up like medieval dwellings beneath the walls of a huge pink castle. Very early next morning, Elizabeth was given the job of carrying it into Kate's room while the rest of us woke her up by singing *Happy Birthday*. I couldn't remember Kate, or indeed any of us, ever having a party breakfast in bed and she was gracious enough to be overwhelmed. Perhaps, now that she knew she was leaving to get married, she felt she could be more generous to Helena. For myself, I just wanted these charming and sentimental delights to go on for ever; and felt, with Helena in our midst, that they actually could.

That night, the new roof room reverberated to the biggest crowd we had ever had in the house: our friends from school, Kate's friends from Alnwick, Richard's friends from the surrounding farms, and people I scarcely knew. It was very noisy and drunken, with pop records and modern dancing, and there were times when Dad looked truly bewildered by it all. To add to the heady brew of excitement and poignancy, Kate's engagement was officially announced and Richard produced the ring. He put it on her finger with a romantic flourish we had not quite expected from him, to a somewhat bawdy response from the crowd. Helena, cheerful but appparently completely sober, revealed herself as the tirelessly efficient hostess we had imagined. I joined Dad for a quiet moment on the stairs.

"I'm whacked," he grinned. "This must be what they mean by middle age. I'm losing a daughter and gaining a beer-cellar…or rather a beer-attic. I suppose it's all downhill from here."

"Nonsense, Dad." I hugged his arm; something I had seen Helena do. Now it seemed quite natural for me to do it, too. "You're enjoying it really."

"You'll be next, I imagine," Dad tweaked my nose, "you and Alan with his souped-up car."

"Oh no, Alan's not the husband for me. He's just a friend."

"Well, make sure you get a few more driving lessons on the airfield before you throw him over."

"I'm not going to throw him over, Dad, but I'm not going to marry him either."

"Looking for Mister Right, eh?"

"No. I'm not going to go looking for Mister Right. He can come looking for me while I train to be an actress."

"Ah, all worked out I see."

"Helena says she'll help me get into Drama School in London after I've left school here. She knows some people who might help. Oh, don't look so miserable, Dad…it'll not be for ages yet, and I'll be back whenever I can and always in the holidays, you know that."

He kissed me on the forehead.

"We'll all come and see you when you're famous and I'll be able to point you out on the television."

"For Heaven's sake Dad, I'm not even in yet. It's just a plan."

"You'll carry it off, though," he smiled, "I know. I'm proud of you, Julie. Of all my daughters, you've done the most to help me and Helena. You know that, don't you? To tell you the truth—and you deserve the truth—when Helena came along, she and I thought you might be the one who took it the hardest; you know, felt the most upset by the changes."

"Because I'm supposedly at the most awkward age?"

"Something like that."

"It turned out to be Kate instead."

"Yes," he chuckled, running his fingers through his hair. "Well, she's going now, and it won't be so difficult for her. She sees how things are now, I know she does. I didn't want her to go unhappy, and I don't think she is—not now that she understands."

"She's got a new life as well," I stated.

"That's right. We all have a new life. She didn't miss out on one after all; in fact she has two new lives now, hasn't she? One with us and one with Richard. She can move between them whenever she likes. I'd say that was pretty good, wouldn't you?"

"I love you, Dad."

* * *

Yet even this was not enough. I knew there was something else I had to accept and put into practice...and I didn't manage to do it until after Kate's wedding.

It was a baking hot day towards the very end of the Summer holidays, the sky completely cloudless, the sun filling it with a brightness so fierce that I was wearing sunglasses, which I hardly ever wore. An early harvest was in progress, the farmers making the most of a dry spell that could end any day. We girls always tried to walk round the old airfield at least once during each harvest so we could watch the rabbits and mice, and sometimes the voles, weasels and stoats, as they scurried out of the corn while it was being cut. But this year I was alone, and I hadn't really come to look for the animals. I had come just to be on my own, to rediscover the real person I knew to be inside myself, somehow free from all the wrangling we had been through in this crazy year, tired of it yet made by it.

The long runways were empty, but they were washed by sound: the distant growl of traffic on the A1, the closer rattle of the combine-harvesters as they hissed and roared through the cornfields like ungainly ships leaving wakes of dust across a sea of wheat. The air was filled with the hot, dry scent of the harvest; there was even a faint corn-coloured dust across the grey tarmac where I walked. I pulled off my shoes. The old tarmac was wonderfully hot under my feet; every step was a kind of thrill, as if all the good things of the Earth were caressing me. I thought how beautiful Helena would have looked on this beautiful day, her perfect skin lit by hot sunshine. I realised it might be annoying to some people that everything about Helena seemed so perfect, but I also realised I could never dislike her for it or be jealous of her. To me, her beauty made her more special than ever. Kate, and perhaps the rest of the world—apart from Dad, of course—might not see it that way, but I knew I would never stop admiring her or loving her.

I lay down on the old runway, looking up to the fathomless blue, putting the palms of my hands and soles of my feet on the hot tarmac, feeling the thrust of the Earth under my shoulders and hips. The Universe seemed to roll ahead of me, as if I were flying through space on the very edge of the world…which of course I actually was, but that wasn't a sensation I thought about every day. It was sensuous, liberating, dizzily exciting. I felt I was being stroked by the Earth on my back and by Heaven on my front, and I suddenly wanted to be kissed—not especially by Alan, whose kiss might be boyish and silly and just embarrassing, but by a man I had yet to meet: a lover or a husband still out there somewhere in the roaring blue world. I would be happy to let him come to me, not impatient to meet him, would know him instantly and give myself to him as lightly as closing my eyes to the sun. I thought of Dad's question to Helena: 'Is there anywhere you especially like to be kissed?' which had caused us terrible giggles when we had first heard it, but which I now thought was wonderful and romantic and the question I most wanted to be asked. I decided, with a delicious thrill, that I should most like to be kissed just below my navel, where the sunshine burned hot through my clothes. I imagined being kissed there and caressed all over by the man I had yet to meet. Then I saw myself as beautiful as Helena, although in quite a different way, and understood her love for Dad, and didn't feel threatened or frightened or jealous or angry or anything that Kate had felt. I was just happy for them.

But the one thing left for me to do was still not done. It was to forgive Kate, and so welcome her back into the family as I had welcomed Helena. I had to lead us all back to loving Kate and understanding her, by loving and understanding her myself...after I had been so upset by her not loving or understanding Helena. I remembered what had happened, and reckoned that there was nothing too serious to forgive beyond some displays of bad manners. Kate hadn't really spoiled anything; she hadn't stopped anything happening which was going to happen anyway. She had certainly hurt Helena and the rest of us, but she had surely hurt herself much more. She was the real victim of her own hatred. It dawned on me that those who hate are always the real victims of their own hatred. To hate was ridiculous. It was wasteful, exhausting, and ultimately stupid—whether in a family or between nations. Well, the war was over. I would never tolerate it or think it clever to re-open its wounds. Peace and love were here, just waiting to be celebrated. To forgive, to utterly forgive my elder sister who had annoyed me for years: how difficult that would have seemed even half an hour ago. Now, I knew I could do it. Perhaps I was already doing it; had perhaps even done it in these last few moments. I had learned how from Helena, who had brought so many good things. Perhaps this was the best of all.

Filled with the kind of joy bred only by acceptance and understanding, I stood up, put on my shoes, and walked back to the village. The sun poured down like honey through sweet and heavy air, but could not lay the dust of the harvest, nor still the new stirrings in my soul. I knew I had not yet grown up, but I had begun to understand what it meant to be a woman.

The End

About the Author

Poet, novelist and scriptwriter Roger Harvey was born in 1953 and lives in Newcastle. His books include the novels *Percy the Pigeon*, *The Silver Spitfire* and *A Woman Who Lives by the Sea* and the poetry collections *Raising the Titanic*, *Divided Attention* and the award-winning *Northman's Prayer*. His published plays include *Asra! Asra!*, about the secret love-life of Samuel Taylor Coleridge and the black farce *Money! Money! Money!* His play *Guinevere-Jennifer* was made into a film. *Poet on the Road* is the intimate travelogue of a U.S.A. Tour. Recent releases include *Albatross Bay*, *River of Dreams*, *The Green Dress and Other Stories* and *The Writing Business*. He is married to Sheila Young, an expert on Royal jewellery whose book *The Queen's Jewellery* became the definitive work on the subject. His other interests include music, photography, and classic cars. For more information about Roger and his work please visit www.roger-harvey.co.uk.